CATTY-CORNERED

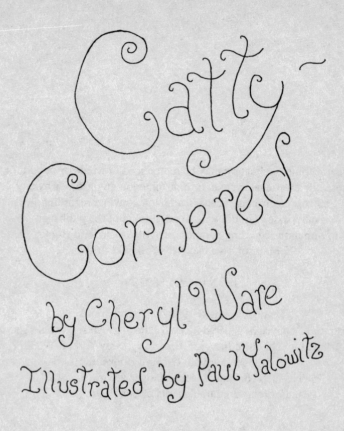

Catty-Cornered

by Cheryl Ware

Illustrated by Paul Yalowitz

SCHOLASTIC INC.

New York Toronto London Auckland Sydney
Mexico City New Delhi Hong Kong

ISBN 0-439-28893-2

12 11 10 9 8 7 6 5 4 3 2 1   1 2 3 4 5 6/0

Printed in the U.S.A.   40

First Scholastic printing, March 2001

The text of this book is set in 12 point Usherwood Book.
The illustrations are pen and ink.
Book design by Mina Greenstein

For Lillie and Rosa, my grandmothers
—C.W.

STOP!

This is the journal of

Venola Mae Cutright.

Do not enter !!!

No humans, brothers, or CATS

allowed !

Day One: "Trapped in Grannyland"

If you are reading this, you are in big trouble, Bobby Cutright! This is my PERSONAL diary, and I will tell Mama about the collection of girlie magazines under your bed.

Since Granddad died last week everything has been crazy. Relatives staying, sleeping on the floor—Uncle Raymond snores even louder than Daddy. Now it's been decided that I am going to stay nights with Grandma—no one even asked me!

Grandma has 46 grandchildren. WHY was I the one chosen to spend nights with her? My sparkling personality? My dazzling smile? Ha. Ha.

I'm not that special. I'm not even pretty. I'm tall, skinny, and have stringy straight brown hair. My sister Katrina is blond and gorgeous, AND closer to Grandma's age.

I snore and have BAD breath in the morning. Katrina sleeps like a quiet little angel, and never makes anyone gag if she breathes on them first thing.

I'm not even fun to be with. Katrina can twirl a baton, tap-dance, and do the macarena. I trip if

I try to chew bubble gum and walk at the same time. They are making a BIG mistake.

Maybe I wouldn't mind staying with Grandma if it wasn't for the cats. 13 of them! Mama and Daddy say Grandma is afraid to stay alone. I don't see how anyone with 13 cats qualifies as being alone, especially with Princess, the black Siamese she-devil, clawing you in the back of the leg. But, Mama and Daddy aren't budging on my "technically, she's-not-alone" theory.

List of things I can do at Grandma's to keep from going completely crazy:

1. Play with the cats. (Ha. Ha.)
2. Watch TV. (Nope, Grandma only watches the religious shows. MTV is out.)
3. Call Sally. (No phone in Granddad's room! Plus Sally can't get calls after eight.)
4. Do my homework. (Yeah, right. Well, maybe on school nights, but on weekends? Get real.)
5. Plan revenge against my brother Bobby for all the mean things he says to me.
6. Sneak out and become an international spy or something exciting. (I guess this would be cheating because I'd be leaving Grandma alone. I'd probably end up getting grounded. Hmmmm. If I get grounded, I

wonder if I would have to stay home
instead of with Grandma???)
7. I could at least READ about international spies
    and stuff. (Well, only until nine because
    Grandma turns her lights out early, and Mama
    and Daddy don't want me running her
    electric bill sky-high.)
8. Write in my journal. I probably will do lots of
    this. I could write down all my hostility
    about having to come up here. I'll probably
    go broke buying journals to write down
    everything, but at least I'll remember it all
    better so I can talk to a therapist when I
    grow up. That is, IF I grow up and the dumb
    cats don't decide to smother me in my
    sleep. There's something about how they
    follow me with their sneaky, squinty little
    eyes I just don't trust.

   P.S. If I keep a journal, and the cats DO kill me,
maybe my writing will help the detectives
pinpoint exactly which one of the fleabags had it
in for me.
   P.P.S. Did I mention that I do not particularly
care for horses, ferrets, parrots, fish, tarantulas,
turtles, gerbils, gorillas, goats, hamsters, guinea
pigs, and especially CATS?
   P.P.P.S. That goes for fleas, too!

P.P.P.P.S. I like dogs.

P.P.P.P.P.S. Bobby, I've warned you once. If I catch you reading this, I'll give Mama the list I've been keeping of all the bad things you've done since I've been old enough to write. (Two spiral notebooks full and growing daily!)

Grandma goes to bed at 7:30 p.m. Sharp. Ahhhhhh! I can't go to sleep that early. It's still kind of daylight out. This is the worst.

Mama says, "Going to bed earlier will be good for you. Kids need their rest for school."

HA! I've been staying awake watching scary late movies as far back as I can remember, and my school work isn't suffering. I don't fall asleep in class (any more than the next person—and lots less than Sammy Potter). I've made it to seventh grade, and I'm holding my own!

Tonight Chilly Billy's <u>Monsterpiece Theater</u> is showing "Attack of the Giant Potato," and I've got to miss it. Sally is going to watch it and tell me the good parts, but it's not the same. I don't like the idea of my best friend seeing an extra vegetable attack the world. So far we were even. Attack of Tomato, Onion, and Rutabaga. It's not fair!

I wonder how you kill a giant potato? Cover its eyes and trick it into a giant microwave? Mash it? Ha. Ha.

Tonight when I was leaving to walk up through
the field to Grandma's, Mama said, "Now Venola
Mae, you be especially nice to your Granny because
she's grieving. She lived with Granddaddy for 65
years, and now he's not there anymore. How would
you feel?"

I couldn't tell her how I really feel—that I'd lived
with her, Daddy, Katrina, Philip, Melvin, James,
and Bobby for almost 12 years, and now they had
gone and shoved me out, and I was grieving for
them, too (and their TV).

Well, maybe not for Bobby.

I couldn't tell her that I don't miss Granddad very
much at all. How could I miss him? I didn't even
know him. Most of my life, Grandma and Grandad
lived out in the country, and we only visited
them every other month or so. During those visits,
I spent most of my time with my cousins and
brothers down at the creek catching crawdads and
playing king of the mountain.

Granddad was scary, like a troll in bedtime
stories. In his old house, he spent a lot of time
out in the garden or in his bedroom, a dark dungeon
with an army blanket hung for a door and a

tobacco spit can by his unmade bed. (I know about the spit can because I knocked it over once when he sent me for his reading glasses. GAG!) Granddad was about seven feet tall and skinny as a scarecrow who'd been left out in the field too long. The thing I remember most about him was his pointy chin. It stuck out so far, it could have put someone's eye out. Daddy's does a little bit, but not as much as Granddad's.

(Yikes! Does mine stick out?!? Right now it is $1\frac{1}{4}$ inches from my bottom lip to the tip of my chin. I wonder if people think I'm as pointy as Granddad and are too nice to say anything.)

Then last year the strip-mine people made Granddad and Grandma move off the land they rented, the land they'd lived on all their lives, and they came to live in our backyard. Mama and Daddy bought a trailer for them, a brand-new two-bedroom one, with avocado green carpet, curtains, and appliances. (It's the first green refrigerator and stove I've ever seen. I thought they just came in white, except for the ones at school, which are silver and HUGE enough to walk in. But we're not allowed. I asked the cooks.)

Once Granddad and Grandma moved into town, he sat outside in our yard by the big oak tree looking lost. He tried to put us littler grandkids on his lap to tell us stories. (Not Katrina, because

her big butt would probably have crushed his legs!)
Granddad's wrinkled arthritic hands looked like
they belonged to a hitchhiker trying to go both
directions at the same time.

Even my brothers tried to avoid him and his
World War I stories. I <u>might</u> have stayed around
and listened if he had told <u>ME</u> about his war
experiences, but when I walked up he always
changed the subject, saying, "Those times ain't
proper for the company of ladies. I'll finish telling
you later, boys."

This made me madder than if he'd hit me
between the eyes with his spit can. I'm sure I've
heard grosser things than he could come up with
in a million years.

Take for example when Mama and Grandma
and all my aunts get together. The conversation can
get downright disgusting. I think they try to one
up each other with the pain and gory details of
their deliveries—even at the supper table. They
pass words like "placenta," "C-section," and
"umbilical cord" around the table right along
with the corn and mashed potatoes. No kidding.
They sling sentences across the table at each
other like "I just dropped in the wheelchair, and
those nurses had to hold Venola's head until they
could get me into the delivery room."

Aunt Louise can't wait for someone to start

talking childbirth so she can bring up her own war story: "Oh honey, you were lucky. I spent 36 hours in them stirrups, sucking on ice. That's all they'd give me until Frederick was born."

Surely Granddad must have been deaf if he'd missed out on these colorful conversations. How in the world could he think I was all fragile and innocent with all <u>that</u> going on? But that's okay because like I said, he was kind of scary and I probably wouldn't have spent much time with him anyhow.

My grandma's name is "Lily," which is kind of cool since my other grandma's name is Rosa. I wish my mama would have named me a flower name like Lilac Sunshine Cutright or Lavender Meadow Cutright or even Holly Chrysanthemum, but no-O-o. She had to be all traditional and name me after her two grandmothers—Venita Mae and Murola Virginia. Ugh.

I may change my name if I can come up with a good one. Girls at school are changing the spelling of their names, and others have come up with new names altogether. Missy Fowler has started spelling her name "Missie" so that she can have two little hearts above her name. Carla Smith has started spelling her name with a "K." She says it's more sophisticated, and she won't pass notes back if you spell it the old-fashioned "C" way.

Sally wants to be "Nicole," but Mrs. Stemple, our homeroom teacher, won't call her that, even though Sally corrects her all the time. Mrs. Stemple says it has to be changed legally at the courthouse, and then she will call Sally "Mud" if she wants her to. Who would want to be called "MUD"?

I asked Mama to take me to the courthouse to change my name to Lavender. She just laughed. Then I asked her if she would just call me "Lavender" around the house, and maybe it would grow on her. She just laughed AGAIN and said only if I call her "Queen of the Morning Glories." I did, but she just gave me one of those "Don't-Push-It" looks.

FLOWER NAMES

* Lavender *   Lilac

Fern
       Blossom   Clover
Marigold   Dahlia
         Daisy   Tiger Lily

Iris   Mum

    Ivy   Scarlet   Sage *

Lotus   * Jasmine *   Pansy
                                (Nope!)   Rose
              Petunia
     Carnation (No Way!)
                                          Orchid
                        Tulip

I think Grandma's been remaking my bed every morning. It's always neater than how I leave it. She's real neat and tidy. Everything has a place.

I must take after Granddad—minus the spit can, that is. I like all my books, clothes, and stuff on my dresser, or on the floor where I can see them. It's easier to find things that way.

Grandma has lots of pictures of grandkids, knickknacks, and LOTS of potted plants all arranged in perfect order. Not a speck of dust anywhere.

At first, I wondered why my grandparents had separate rooms, but one good look at Granddad's mess would explain to anyone. I bet it was the only way Grandma could live in the same house with the slob without murdering him.

Oooh. I guess I shouldn't say that even if he was a slob, since I'm sleeping in HIS room. In HIS bed. The one he died in! Do you think part of him is still here? At the funeral Reverend Lawson said something about Granddad continuing to watch over us. I wouldn't want to make any restless spirits mad. He was scary enough when he was alive. As soon as it gets dark, my flashlight's going on. Bobby says night-lights are for babies, but I say they are for people who have to sleep in their dead granddad's bed. Help.

Note to self: Buy lots of batteries tomorrow. (There goes this week's profit from the paper route.)

Too tired to write much. Missie was meaner than usual today.

1. She told Sammy Potter that I am in love with him, and so he started throwing paper wads at me.
2. She told Karla that I told her that Karla looked fat. (Missie is the one who said it. I just didn't disagree.)
3. AND, she dropped (ON PURPOSE) one of the notes I wrote to her about Mrs. Stemple's run in her pantyhose. (I just said that maybe she should buy queen size and then they wouldn't rip all the time.)
4. I got detention hall for writing the note AND a lecture on keeping my mind on schoolwork. Mine was only one of a hundred bazillion notes passed today, and Mrs. Stemple acted as if I wrote the first one in the history of Belington Middle School. I thought teachers were supposed to have eyes in the backs of their heads, but obviously Mrs. Stemple is blind except when it comes to me doing something wrong!!!

Boy was she mad. Her voice got real high and hurt my ears. "Some people are here to learn, Miss Cutright, and they do not appreciate your elementary school antics. I'll not have this kind of chaos brewing in my classroom."

Yikes! Did she think I was going to single-handedly start a note-passing cult and make the rest of the class do something crazy like shave their heads or watch TV instead of doing their homework???

P.S. Missie purred out an apology at lunch in front of Sally, but she was smiling. "I can't believe I dropped your note. I guess it fell out of my jacket pocket when I got up to go to the bathroom." Then she gave me her loveliest smile again. Oooooh.

Note to self: Punish Missie.

Grandma formally introduced me to each and every one of her babies today. She said it more than likely hurt their feelings when I just said "Hey cat" as I passed one of them in the hall. I think they're lucky to get a "Hey cat!" from a confessed cat-hater like me. But I humored her.

So I said, "Hello, Princess." (Prissy Princess expects to be greeted first and with enthusiasm, or she swats you one. And she still has her claws!)

Grandma doesn't believe in declawing animals. When I asked her if she'd ever considered the procedure for her cats, she said, "If God didn't want them to scratch things, he wouldn't have given them claws. It's not natural to take that away from a poor defenseless little animal." I think her couch might have a different opinion from the looks of it.

The rest of the cats aren't as fussy and don't require individual greetings. Gran says the order doesn't matter, and I can probably lump them together without getting attacked. I guess they are used to Princess's aristocratic rules. (I wonder if Princess and Missie Fowler are related!)

I played along with Gran the best I could. "Hey,

Old Blue, Tom, Chester, Sylvester, Baby, Shoeshine, KitKat, Incadinkadoo (don't ask me!), Boogie, Hank, Tennessee Ernest, and Patsy Cline."

Don't ask me to name them again tomorrow. Yes, I've got lots of brothers to remember, but nothing like Gran's clan. I hope she doesn't quiz me on them. Maybe I could make up one of those sentences to remember things like Miss Corley taught us in music class. <u>Every good boy does fine.</u> I remember the sentence, even if I don't remember what it stands for.

Princess   Old Blue
Tom   Chester
Sylvester
Kit Kat   Baby
                  Incadinkadoo
Boogie   Shoeshine
Hank   Tennessee Ernest
Patsy Cline

~~People ought to come to school~~

People of Belington taste chicken ~~several~~ some

beets, ketchup xxxxxxxxxxxxxx

Hmmm . . . Maybe backward. . . .

19

Can Princess eat three hairy, stinky bugs in
? ? ? ? ? ? ? ? ? ? ?

Pampered cats should be kept in pantry closets to
eat hair balls or snakes, bugs, (and) toads.

Getting sleepy. Maybe tomorrow I'll make a
better sentence. Not as easy as I thought.

Princess jumped off the refrigerator onto
Grandma's back, nearly knocking her down.
Grandma just laughed and told her she was a
"little itty-bitty silly kitty." (More like a vicious
carnivore with fangs and five-inch claws. I guess
love is blind.)

Note to self: Do not go near refrigerator no matter
how thirsty you get in the middle of the night!

Today at school I got the bright idea to ask Sally if she would stay nights with me at Grandma's sometimes.

She said, "No way. I think I'm allergic to cats—especially thirteen all at once."

"Well, I was just thinking you might miss your own grandparents since they live so far away," I said.

Her grandparents up and moved to Florida last year, and Sally was really upset and cried a lot. But apparently she had gotten over it without me knowing it.

She said, "Sometimes I guess I miss them. But there's a lot of perks to having long-distance grandparents. They miss you and send really neat presents all the time, and you can visit the beach during Thanksgiving and Christmas vacation!"

So much for Sally's company at Grandma's.

P.S. Do cats like the beach? Maybe I could talk
Grandma into retiring to Florida.

I wonder if cats can tell when someone doesn't like them or their stinking fleas. Tonight they all sat around staring at me, the invader. Then Princess came over and curled up on my lap with the strangest little smile. I'm pretty sure her eyes were saying, "I'll teach you to come up here and pretend to like cats when you really don't. I'm going to sit here as long as I want, and you can't do a thing about it or you'll offend your nice, sweet grandma."

I believe all the other cats were laughing, too. Two more brown striped ones started rubbing against my legs. Bump, bump, bump went their heads into my legs, and GROSS! they left something slimy behind. Cat snot???

I almost gagged.

Grandma said, "Oh look, they like you. They want you to rub their foreheads."

Yeah, right.

Note to self: Don't wear shorts to Grandma's.

Why would anyone want to keep 13 cats in a 12-by-50-foot trailer? This woman parted with most of her belongings when she moved to Belington, but she wouldn't part with a single one of her "babies."

I think she likes the cats better than people. She sure does spend more on cat food than she does on herself! Sometimes I think Grandma forgets to eat. She is losing weight and was too skinny to start with.

Maybe opening the disgusting cat food makes her lose her appetite. I don't know how she can get near some of it, like the Seafood Surprise, without puking. The Feisty Feline turkey isn't that bad. NO, I haven't tasted it, but it smells better than Thanksgiving dinner at school. (But I guess that's not saying much.)

Things aren't actually too bad once you cross the green carpet and start down the linoleumed hall toward Granddad's old room. Then it just smells like Pinesol. Grandma never allowed her babies in Granddad's room because it was too dangerous.

"The cats won't be bothering you none," she said. "They won't venture into your granddaddy's room. God rest his soul, he was mostly a good man, but he despised my babies, didn't he, Princess? Whacked you with his cane every chance he got, but you were just too fast for him, weren't you, Sweetie?"

Hearing this made me think I should have been nicer to Granddad.

Said "hello" to Gran (AND the you-know-whats). Hurried down the hall to avoid Gran's Sunday evening television program. She likes the local station's religious show—complete with the nasal-twang, beehive-hair singers and their tone-deaf, polyester leisure suit band. Yuck.

And Mama says <u>my</u> music makes her ears bleed! She should spend Sunday evening with Grandma, who just happens to be a bit hard of hearing and who likes to listen to her favorite programs a tad on the loud side.

MTV is only two tiny channels away. So close but yet so far! I'd settle for VH-1. The country station, almost! Something tells me Grandma's not going to compromise on this one. She's got that look on her face that Dad and my brothers get when they watch Saturday night <u>Wrestling Mania.</u> Zombie City.

P.S. I think the cats are siding with me. Of course Patsy Cline and Tennessee Ernest are still wailing along with Granny and the choir, but the rest of Granny's little angels are hiding out in the bathroom, and Baby and Old Blue had the nerve to slip under my bed until God finds it in His heart to make those singers STOP. I'd throw the fleabags out of my room, but not even I am that mean to poor defenseless animals. So much for the cats' fear of Granddad's room!

P.P.S. Tonight when Grandma opened the door for me, she said, "Hello, Katrina." What an insult. I am the one giving up my television shows to stay all night with her. At least she could get my name right and not get me confused with Big Butt!!!

Not feeling so good. Didn't mind going to bed
so early for a change.

Today at Kmart Mama bought the new kind of
strawberry essence shampoo, the same kind that
Sally uses. So I figured as pretty as Sally's hair is,
I might as well give it a shot.

Mmmmmm. It smelled just like my favorite Jolly
Rancher candy. So, you guessed it. I tasted it. I
should have just put my tongue to it, but like I said,
it smelled terrific, so I swigged it. Ugh. I'm afraid
to drink anything else tonight, even water, or I
might start burping bubbles. I didn't hurl—yet.
But the night is young.

P.S. The cats better stay out of the way between
me and the bathroom if they know what is good
for them.

P.P.S. I didn't tell Mama about the shampoo
incident because I didn't want to take away
Bobby's record for doing the stupidest thing in the
family. He stuck a Skittle up his nose when he
was seven and had to be rushed to the emergency
room because Mama's tweezers wouldn't quite
reach it. Mama said the pinto bean James stuffed

up his nose wasn't as slippery and wasn't as much trouble to get ahold of, so he is only in second place in our family's "stupid thing" hall of fame. I don't think tasting shampoo even compares to sticking food up your nose, unless it kills me tonight and they figure it out in the autoposy when they open me up and I smell yummy strawberry fresh inside. If the shampoo does kill me, I guess I was wrong about it not being really stupid, and then Bobby can gloat.

P.P.P.S. Why can't Mama buy stinky, flowery shampoo like other moms! Or even the green apple kind. I wouldn't have been tempted by that.

The dumb strawberry stuff didn't make my hair look any better anyway. It's as stringy as ever. Maybe even more, if that is possible.

P.P.P.P.S. If the shampoo does kill me tonight, will the cats crawl all over me? Ahhhh. I think I'll sleep with my head under the covers just in case.

For other kids, this 7:30 bedtime might not be so bad, but I'm an admitted TV addict and pretty much have to be pushed out my own family's door.

I've started blaming Granny for my missed TV shows. At school today Sally mentioned last night's episode of The Nanny, and I was so jealous my face probably glowed greener than the witch's on the The Wizard of Oz. It was a Nanny I hadn't seen before, too!

No one at my house seems to care when I complain about having to go to Grandma's so early. Just two weeks ago I was a kid used to staying awake past midnight, and now everyone thinks I can go to sleep by 7:30??? I DON'T THINK SO.

P.S. It IS easier to wake up in the morning since I started going to bed early. Mama used to have to drag me out of bed. Sometimes I wake up before Gran's alarm goes off now.

Today Gran said, "You're starting to get up with the roosters. You're going to put them out of a job." Great! I've found my calling. Grandma's training me for a career as a wake-up rooster. No matter what, I'll refuse to cockadoodledoo!

Something weird's happening to my arms. I've got all this fuzzy hair growing on them. It gives me the creeps. When I get cold it stands straight up, and I look like a plucked chicken. What if it grows long enough that I have to start braiding it?

Mr. Coswell probably could braid his. Sometimes in math lab when he comes around and is helping me with a problem, I can't concentrate for looking at his arms. They are hairier than Chester and Sylvester put together, but closer to Old Blue's color. What if the hair on my arms grows like his? Maybe it is already happening. I wonder if I caught it off him. Could abnormal arm hair growth be contagious? If so, I may have to wear long sleeves forever—even in the summer. I might never be able to wear any of my favorite T-shirts again.

Cher was on <u>Oprah</u> talking about electrolysis last week. Maybe I should send away for a brochure or transcript or something before this stuff gets out of hand. Should I order a copy for Mr. Coswell, too? Or would he be offended?

P.S. On the bright side, my arm hair no matter how long will probably be lifeless and flat just like the hair on my head. Mr. Coswell's is really curly and stands up above his watchband. (I bet he screams when he takes off his watch at night. Or maybe his watch is waterproof and he just leaves it on all the time. I'll have to try to get a glimpse of it tomorrow, if I can find it through all the hair.)

P.P.S. I think one of the cats peed under the bed or somewhere. It STINKS in here. I smelled it as soon as I walked in tonight. I know I should tell Grandma, but I'm afraid it would hurt her feelings. Can't she smell it? Ugh.

I read in the newspaper about a woman who raises potbellied pigs and potty trains them. Please don't let Grandma see this article! Meowing and clawing are bad enough. I don't want to have to deal with oinking and grunting.

September 9

Sally's and my experiment failed. Sally tried to give me a hairdo like hers, but according to her, "You need a permanent wave before it will stand up HALF as fluffy and pretty as mine." Hey, just because she's my best friend doesn't mean that she's not a little conceited. But I don't think she meant anything by it. She DOES have beautiful hair, and she was just trying to help me with my straw.

Sally's also downright determined (stubborn) when she wants to be, and so she tried to force my hair to conform with a whole bunch of her mom's fancy mousses, hair spray, electric crimper, and curling iron.

"Ouch," I screamed for the fifteenth time.

"Hold still, Venola Mae Cutright, or I may just burn your whole ear off!" Sally definitely needs to work on her beautician's manners and her first-aid treatments if she's going to try to go into the business professionally—which I do NOT recommend.

When she FINALLY finished, she took the hand mirror and showed me the back and sides just like they do in the beauty parlor. "Not bad, huh?"

She didn't have to walk home! I looked like the

35

Bride of Frankenstein's pet WEREWOLF. Bobby
asked me if I stuck my finger in a light socket and
stepped in a mud puddle at the same time. (As
if he looks any better!)

But don't worry. I know how to get even with
the likes of him. I reminded Mama it was past
time to give the boys haircuts.

"Hey, Bobby, what's wrong with your neck? Did
you hurt it playing ball?" I said real innocent and
concerned to Bobby in Mama's company.

"Nothing, Pukeface. Why?"

"You're just holding your head a little funny,
tilted to one side—maybe your bangs are just
bothering you. Never mind." That's all it took. Tee
hee. He got in trouble for calling me a name
AND was at the front of the line when she got out
her clippers.

He muttered something about paybacks, but I
had to come up here to Gran's, so I reckon I'm
safe till morning. It's not like he can shave my head
in the night or put bubble gum in my hair (like
he did before). He claimed he didn't and that I
probably fell asleep with it in my mouth, but I'm
not convinced. I had to cut a big hunk of hair out
of the side of my head. What a way to start sixth
grade. Mama wanted to even it out and give me
something she called a "pixie," but I told her I
would wear it in a ponytail (and did until I got to

school). The kids said it looked cool and daring, just like the models on fashion shows. That was the only thing I think Sally has ever envied about me. She said that I looked "way nervy."

The teachers didn't say anything at all, but they all looked at me kind of funny for a couple of weeks.

P.S. Cat smell is getting stronger. I used to notice a little funny smell for a few minutes after I came in, but now it's starting to take my breath away. Gotta do something.

1. Covered my head, but nearly suffocated.
2. Thought about putting a clothespin on my nose, but it would hurt, and I was afraid it might make my nose grow. That's all I need is a bigger, longer nose to go with my pointy Cutright chin. (It is still $1\frac{1}{4}$ inches. At least it's not growing fast.)

Kind of glad to slip away to Gran's tonight. Hard to look Mama and Daddy in the eye. (Long story.) But it's only 7:35 p.m. (Still daylight!), so I guess I have time to go into it.

First, remember the hair growing on my arms that I told you about? It was making me crazy, and I was tired of looking like a chimpanzee or a warthog. Every time I got goose bumps on my arms, those hairs would stand at attention faster than any army. How embarrassing. I tried plucking them out, but OUCH! Too many.

Then I was washing up, getting ready to go on my paper route, when I saw the answer to my problem right in front of me—Daddy's razor.

Nobody was home, so I reached for his shaving cream, lathered my arms, and slid the razor up and down (real careful because I'd seen Daddy with little wads of bloody toilet paper on his face!).

I was almost finished and maybe I was hurrying or maybe the razor just slipped, but I cut my arm, right below my elbow. At first it didn't bleed, and I thought "oops" and kept shaving. But then blood started to seep out from underneath my skin. I ran cold water over it real quick to wash off the shaving cream, and it stung bad, REALLY REALLY bad. So I wrapped toilet paper around it, and started crying and saying, "Oh no, oh no, oh no. I'm going to die. I'm going to die. I'm going to die." The more scared I got, the faster it bled, so I wrapped it real tight in some gauze I found and stretched out on the bathroom floor hoping if I settled down some, it would stop bleeding. After a while, it seemed to, so I went on the route (after cleaning up the evidence).

I was doing okay, and then right before I got to the Hi/Lo Store, I got all weak-kneed and light-headed, so I stopped to get a Dr Pepper and some M&M's to build up my strength. Well, I must have looked pretty pale and pitiful because Sammy Potter was in the store and he asked me if I had just seen a ghost.

Then he saw the bandage on my arm. "What happened to you?"

Was I supposed to tell him that I was becoming a hairy werewolf and got cut trying to hide the signs? That's just what I need spread all over school.

I guess my delay as I searched for an alternate story (LIE) that would account for the bandage must have passed for confusion or amnesia.

"Venola, are you okay? You are acting weirder than usual, if that's possible. You aren't going to hurl or pass out or something are you?" He took a step between me and his bike, which was leaning against the store window. I think he wanted to make sure that I didn't hurt IT if I fainted.

I looked at his bike, and the perfect excuse came to me. "Yeah, I'm okay. Just had a bike wreck."

Sammy glanced over at my unscratched brand-new bike I just bought with my route money.

I turned up the Dr Pepper and took a long, slow drink while I thought. "Didn't hurt the bike. It was just a little wreck, and I would have been just fine, too, if I hadn't landed on a broken bottle."

"Ooh, that had to hurt," he said. "Can I see the cut?"

Gross! Who in his right mind wants to see someone's gaping wound? I told him that he was repulsive, but he just threw his Twinkies wrapper at me.

Fooling Sammy wasn't so bad though. He's played plenty of tricks on me. The worst part is I was afraid of what Mama and Daddy would do. They might never leave me alone again until I am 103, so I told them the story about wrecking my bike and running a piece of glass in my arm. The same lie twice in one day. I'm becoming as evil as Missie.

I feel awful (mentally and physically). I'm probably scarred for life. A career in modeling

is definitely out. And also in the FBI because lie
detectors will catch me for what I truly am.

Note to self: Stay away from razors even if your
arms become so hairy they have to lock you up
in a zoo!

I know I'm being a pain in the butt, but I can't
help it. Tonight, I told Mama I'm afraid to walk
in the dark to Grandma's by myself.

"Venola Mae Cutright, what in the world are you
talking about? In the summer you play hide and
seek and cartoon tag out in that yard with your
friends until I finally have to come out and drag
you in."

"I know, but I've been reading some scary things
in the newspaper and one was about a murderer
who claims to be a vampire and sucks the necks
of his vic—"

"Oh, get your things. I'll walk you," she says
before I could even start in on all the details. I
think she knew I was pretending, but she also knew
that Grandma would be waiting and that I could
go on for quite a while.

Hair is coming back on my arms. It's all prickly.
I'm depressed. I feel like a porcupine. Mama noticed
when our arms bumped in the car and asked me
what in the world I did to my arms. I played
dumb, but she just looked at me like I was from
another planet.

P.S. I wonder what Sammy would say if he found
out the truth about my arms? Would he be mad
at me for lying or die from laughter? Who knows.
He is so completely strange that I don't even
care what he thinks! Today he followed me on my
route and called me Granola Mae. How mature!
I've got to think of a good comeback!

Sammy Potter

Bammy   Botter (Bother)
Cammy   Cotter
Dammy   Dotter
Fammy   Fotter

Gammy	Gotter
Hammy	Hotter
Jammy	Jotter
Kammy	Kotter
Krammy	
Lammy	Lotter
Mammy	Motter
Nammy	Notter
	Otter
Pammy	
Rammy	Rotter
Scrammy	Sotter, Snotter
Tammy	Totter (Teeter-Totter)
Whammy	Water
Zammy	Zotter

Darn. Nothing good! Venola Mae is lots easier to make fun of.

Sally planned her wedding today at lunch again.
She's going to marry A.J. in the year 2015.

"I'm going to have an even dozen bridesmaids,"
she said, "all in rose-color taffeta tea-length
gowns, with four-inch heels dyed to match."

"That sounds pretty," I said, hiding a yawn.
(She's had the same twelve bridesmaid plan
since she was old enough to count that high.)

"Well, you'd think my maid of honor would at
least show some enthusiasm."

I guess she saw the yawn. "It's hard to get excited
about four-inch heels when you're already as tall
as Lurch off the <u>Addams Family,</u>" I said, and
slouched down even more in my chair.

"You're not THAT tall."

"Huh! I bet I'll be seven feet by the time you get
married. I'll have to duck to get through the
church door."

All I MEANT was that I was going to grow into
some kind of freak. But Sally only heard "by the
time you get married."

"How do you know when I'll get married? My
wedding will be before yours. You don't even
have a boyfriend!"

Man, all I wanted was to wear flats to her wedding! Sometimes I wonder how we stay friends with all our communication problems.

I don't know why she laughs at my ideas. They aren't any more stupid than hers. I told her that I wanted to get married at the city park on the basketball court because I really like to play there. I'll have a famous cake decorator make a cake in the shape of a basketball court with a cute little couple throwing balls through a net, and then after the wedding, we can have the reception at the picnic tables in the park. Once the cake's gone, we can move the metal chairs and everyone can play basketball—my husband's team against mine. Whoever wins gets to pick where to go for the honeymoon.

Ever since we learned how to make tissue flowers for the sixth-grade basketball tournament decorations, I've planned to use them in my wedding. Sally promised she would help me make flowers out of tissues if I "really had to go through with it," but she said her mom could get me a really good deal on live flowers down at her shop, so as not to embarrass my family and <u>friends.</u> I think tissue corsages would be very useful. The wedding guests may appreciate them and leave better presents. If people start crying (like my mama always does), they could just blow their noses on the flowers. Mama always has to borrow Daddy's hanky.

Sally thinks she is Belington's expert on weddings. She's been in more weddings than any other girl in town because her mom's the only florist in town. When people come in and plan their weddings, if they don't know any girls, Sally's always nice to them and ends up getting invited to be the flower girl. She saves all the old wedding books from her mom's shop, and then we go through them when we are bored.

I cut some interesting weddings out of the newspaper for her sometimes, but she just shakes her head and giggles. I have three all-time favorites. First, the hot-air balloon wedding, except I read about a real sad wedding where the balloon exploded and the bride died. It was tragic, but romantic too. Second, there is the scuba-diving wedding. Two people got married underwater in Aruba. This would not work for me because I cannot swim (only float) and I'm afraid of the water. Third and best was the Halloween wedding. The groom dressed up as Frankenstein and the bride had on a long black dress and white powder on her face. It never really said in the article whether she was trying to be Morticia Addams or the Bride of Frankenstein, but it was really cool and spooky. Sally said it was tacky, but

I myself would rather be in the Halloween wedding than her "A Rose to Remember" theme because those bridesmaids and flower girls got to wear freaky, creative things instead of froufrouy tafetta dresses.

You just can't change some people.

Dreamed Old Blue got married. Grandma was a real nervous mother of the cat, so Mama and I had to help him into his little white dress. (I kept thinking, but he's a boy, but you know how dreams get all goofy and mixed up. So I just zipped him up the back and handed him his bouquet.)

Then Daddy carried Old Blue to the Monte Carlo, so he wouldn't get his dress dirty. Old Blue had a little pink bow in his hair, and looked really adorable. But then we stopped for gas at Sheetz and he escaped, so I bought a Super-Duper-Slurper and then couldn't find a bathroom after I drank the whole thing. Everyone was looking for Old Blue so we wouldn't be late for the wedding, except me. I was looking for a bathroom, but they were all for "Men Only."

I was just about ready to give up and sneak in, when I woke up. I had to hurry to the bathroom, but I made it. Isn't it weird how you dream about something, and then it's in your real world, too? Well, not the wedding dress. You know what I mean.

Every time I look at Old Blue now, I think of him in that little white lacy wedding dress. The last time, he caught me staring at him and hissed. I wonder if cats can read minds???

The fair is coming to town. Two more days. I'm going to ride the Twister and the Scrambler just like last year. I don't know if I'm ready for the Whirl-A-Bullet. Last time I got up there and started smelling all that grease from the concession stand, and bam, I lost my cookies . . . well, corn dogs. (Four.)

Sammy Potter was really nice to me in science class today because I dissected the fish for our group. (Is this the same guy who wanted to look at my cut? WIMP! For a while, I thought he was going to toss a few cookies himself!)

Maybe he will hang out with me and Sally at the fair and ride with us. I don't care if he doesn't. But it would be okay if he did. I guess. If he doesn't call me Granola, that is.

Grandma says I can have my pick of her quilt collection for my bed at her house! Plus she's going to buy curtains to match.

"It's time we give this room a touch of Venola Mae pizzazz!" she said. "Your granddad was color-blind and didn't give a hoot what old quilt I tossed over his bed. Just so it was plenty warm."

I'll give Grandma credit for that. She's got lots better taste than Granddad. I've always liked to look at Grandma's stuff, especially her quilts—even at the old house I peeked into her bedroom every chance I got. It was my favorite place in their whole house, and not just because she didn't have a gross spit can beside her bed to trip over. Her room was bright and breezy with a white tulip spread covering her neat little twin bed. She made lots of quilts and folded them over the foot of her bed rail.

All those colors and designs kind of hypnotized me. The first time Grandma caught me admiring her quilt collection, I thought she was going to yell at me for snooping in her room. But she didn't. She just stretched each and every one of those quilts on her bed and named them. She had

Moon over the Mountain, a Wedding Ring, eight-
pointed Starburst, Maple Leaf, Spring Sunrise,
Bumblebee, and my favorite one with little pink,
blue, lilac, and yellow Holly Hobbie girls.

Grandma says we're going to unpack all of her
quilts this weekend so that I can make a decision,
but I know I won't have to think twice. Two words:
HOLLY HOBBIE!!! But I didn't tell Grandma
because I want to look at them all again. (I think
she does, too.)

What happened to the fair this year? They had the same rides, but they looked all rinky-dink. Could they have shrunk? Mama says I'm just growing up.

I don't know, but everything did look dirty and small. (Not the corn dogs.) But the stuffed animals were the same ones they had last year and were all dusty. The Scrambler looked like it might fly apart at any minute. They didn't even have the Whirl-A-Bullet, and the Electric Swings they replaced it with creaked like the chains were ready to break, AND they went out over the river when they were up in the air.

I decided not to take any chances, and spent my money on cotton candy. Sammy did, too. He followed me everywhere, and I thought maybe he liked me, but then his friend Dewayne showed up, and Sam got all weird, and put his cotton candy in my hair.

I am never getting married. I am going to be a very successful career woman and then spend my riches on my own amusement park full of tissue flower gardens with EXCITING rides and my own personal movie theater, and I won't let anyone who is mean to me in. AND I NEVER FORGET!!!!!!

Okay, I did it again. You would think I'd learn my lesson after the razor thing, but No-O-o!

I was watching MTV, and on the House of Style all the really elegant supermodels kept having blond hair—like Sally's.

When I told Mama I wished my hair was like Sally's and her mom's, she said they were "peroxide blonds." From Mama's tone, I knew I couldn't ask Sally if it were true, even if she is my best friend. Because I figured she'd get mad at Mama and me both.

So here I was alone on Sunday afternoon, and I thought, What the heck? And I locked myself in the bathroom with the peroxide. I poured it up real close to the roots, and made sure it didn't run down into my eyes because I know how peroxide foams and bubbles and burns when Mama pours it in my ears to give them a good cleaning out.

Then I washed my hair with that sickening-smelling strawberry shampoo (it hasn't smelled good since I drank it), and went out and sat in the sun for it to dry and turn blond. With my rotten luck, I should have known mine would NOT look like Sally's hair.

This evening at the supper table, Mama said, "Venola Mae Cutright, what did you do to your hair?"

"Washed it, why?" (Okay, that part <u>was</u> true.)

"It's all funny colored, especially on top. Washed-out looking," she said.

I thought it looked a little lighter myself, but it's hard to tell by just looking in the mirror inside. It seemed a little more red than blond, but I kind of liked it, so I started watching a cat food commercial like I was real interested and said to Mama supercasually, "Didn't do anything different. Just used that new shampoo you bought, the kind that smells like strawberries. It kind of burned. I think my head's too sensitive for it."

Yes, I lied again. I wonder if I'm turning into a pathological liar? Was I born this way or is my family driving me to it by confining me to the company of C-A-T-S?!? Ahhhhh!

Gran has a lot of old wives' tales. She told me
tonight about how she cut the teeniest, tiniest
tip off of each cat's tail and buried it under the
porch. She says when you do this, they will never
ever leave.

I bet if I cut their tails all the way off, they would
leave. Just kidding. Anyway, I'd never catch
Princess. She's so fast I'd have to catch her off
guard.

No cats allowed in my room! Last night I dreamed I was in the jungle, swinging a big machete. I kept chanting, "I'm going lion hunting. I'm not afraid." (I'm not making this up! Why would anyone make up a dream about that third-grade song?!?)

Then the ground and trees started rumbling with a terrible growling sound. Out from behind some trees roared Boogie and Baby, bigger than lions. The other cats marched out behind them, two by two, and each two were larger than those in front. I pointed my machete at them, but it turned into a little pair of safety scissors.

I tried to scream, but no sound came out (DON'T YOU HATE THAT?), and then I heard an evil laugh. I knew it right away. There was no mistaking it. PRINCESS. Blacker and shinier than silk, and bigger than an elephant. I knew not to run. She could squash me with one of her paws, or stick me through the stomach with one of her giant claws like a little swedish meatball on a toothpick.

I decided to climb a tree and look her in the eye. I climbed and climbed up a really sharp vine. My hands were bleeding, but I held on to the scissors, determined if I got the chance, I'd cut her tail off so she would leave.

She just kept cackling. I wanted to cover my ears, but I couldn't let go of the vine, so I yelled, "Quit laughing at me!" But when I looked into her eyes, it wasn't Princess.

I said, "Grandma?!?" And she squall-cackled, and swatted me out of the tree.

I fell and fell and fell. Probably 50,000 feet. I just kept falling.

Before I hit the ground, I woke up. Everything was dark and silent, but then I felt it—something walking across my head, chewing on my toes, and clawing at the knotted bits of yarn on the quilts.

Then the trailer reverberated: <u>BAM,</u> "MEOOW!"

Gran heard. "What's wrong?" she called.

"Nothin', Gran. The cats are just playing, ran into a wall," I said as I rubbed my aching foot. Oh boy. I lied again. Honest, I didn't mean to kick the darn cat, but when I jumped out of bed it just kind of went flying.

I swear, it was an accident. But try telling that to a cat. Princess will probably come back and eat my face off tonight.

I know I should feel guilty for forcing Mama and Daddy to walk me around the corner to watch me walk up the path, but I don't.

Tonight when it was time to head up the hill, I said, "Well, I'm going now. Someone'll probably get me on the way to Grandma's, but that's okay. I don't have anything to live for. Can't even watch a TV show all the way through."

No one even blinked. Mama, Daddy, and my brothers' eyes were glued to the television set. They were watching a made-for-TV movie with Valerie Bertinelli as the lead.

"Don't no one bother getting up . . ."

No one moved.

"Well, if you want to walk me up, I guess I could wait for a commercial. I wouldn't want you to miss the good part—"

"We get the point. Let's move," Daddy said.

Daddy rigged up a lightbulb on the clothesline
post today, so I wouldn't have to be afraid of
the dark on my way to Gran's. When I asked anyone
if they were walking with me, Mama said, "I'll
watch you through the window, honey."

"Fine, just wave when someone grabs me in the
dark. You'll be a big help in there. Maybe you
should get the binoculars, so you can give an
accurate description to the police," I muttered
as I walked across our porch and down the steps.

"What are you saying, young lady?"

"Nothing, Mama."

But what I wanted and expected was <u>their</u> feet
to get cold in the dew and <u>their</u> shows to be
interrupted.

Am I an awful person? Don't answer that!

Note to self: Try to be nicer to family, even Bobby.
Not Katrina because she yelled at me for messing
in her makeup. How else am I supposed to learn?
Missie Fowler already wears it, and she looks a
lot older. Sally's mom let her get some blush and
mascara. I am a month older, why can't I?

Gran was taking her hair down when I got to her house tonight. How could anyone grow hair to her knees?

I started wondering if she gets tangled in it when she sleeps. So I said, "Grandma, aren't you afraid of getting all twisted up in your hair in your sleep?"

"Hmmm," she said. "I never really gave it much thought, but I'm probably pretty safe. I've learned how to deal with it over the past 80 years, and I don't think it's a real danger to me now. Plus, I've never heard of death by hair before."

Grandma has a really pretty smile. I sat down and watched her brush her hair out. It sparkles like the morning sun on a fresh snow.

I told her I wished I knew how to do stuff with my hair, and guess what? She showed me. She brushed out all my tangles. (Ouch.) And then braided it for me. In the morning she's going to french braid it. I can't wait until Sally sees. I think it will make me look 15 or 16.

P.S. If I never get my hair cut, I wonder how long it will be by the time I graduate from middle school?

Sally was really, really jealous. She wants to know if Gran can braid her hair, too. I'm not sure she would like all the cats. She <u>is</u> allergic. Maybe she will forget about the whole thing. I like looking different. If she does it, too, then people will quit noticing my braid because Sally is lots prettier. I wish I looked like her. I would become a long-sleeve model. I wonder if my arm is scarred for life???

Warm WEEKEND nights are the worst—for more
than the obvious cat stink reason.

When I open my bedroom window, I can still
hear sounds of life from home. Mama's been
laughing at something for the past half hour. I
wonder if it is <u>America's Funniest Home Videos.</u>
I <u>love</u> that show, even the videos about cats.

AND it's nearly impossible to fall asleep with their
phone ringing off the hook. I wonder if it's
Melvin's girlfriend or Philip's? Definitely not
Bobby's because he is too creepy to have one.
Maybe Katrina is home from her job at Pizza Hut.
I wonder if she brought any pizza home. Maybe
my favorite stuffed crust with pepperoni and green
peppers. Oh no, I'm hungry now. I could
ALMOST eat cat food. Then the cats would kill me
in my sleep for sure.

Reading helps the time pass. Sometimes it's too noisy at home, and I can't concentrate. <u>Paper Moon</u> is a really funny book. I wish I could go off and be a con artist like Addie Pray. She is street-smart, and no one puts anything over on her, not even Long Boy. Mama would kill me if I ever pulled the Bible scam or the wallet drop.

I'd LIKE to keep reading, and see how it ends, but my flashlight must be starting to bother the dumb cats. There's a horde of cats meowing and scratching outside my door, tattling to Granny that something is up at this end of the hall. How's a person supposed to read a book and learn how to become a professional con artist with all these distractions?

Maybe I should try bribing the cats. If they promise to let me read and to keep quiet about me not going to sleep, I could give them little treats. What would make a good cat bribe? Fish sticks? Milk? How am I going to sneak those things in without Grandma noticing? They would swarm me like I was a rock star.

What would Addie Pray and Long Boy do? I bet a couple of con artists could handle a bunch of cats! They would probably sell the cats door to door and tell people they were celebrity cats worth thousands of dollars. Or maybe trade them to a circus for a monkey or some other cool animal.

I'd just get in trouble if I did something like that. PLUS I've been reading that animals can find their way home from ANYWHERE! One cat followed its family from Virginia to California when they moved without it. I bet it had sore feet! I wonder if it was mad at them or just happy to be reunited with its family. I wonder if the family moved again when the cat turned its head.

I'm only allowed to ride my bike across town. The cats would probably beat me back home. I guess the dumb cats are here to stay.

Maybe I could buy some of those little triangle-shaped treats at Shop-N-Save with my paper route money and keep them sealed until I get to my room. I bet that's all it would take to have them eating out of the palm of my hand. Yuck. More cat slime!

No way! I can't believe I'm even considering spending my hard-earned money on the enemy!!! Forget it, I'll just continue cat-hating myself to sleep. It works a lot better than counting sheep. "I hate Princess. I hate Old Blue. I hate Tom. I hate Boogie. I hate Chester and Sylvester. I hate Baby. I hate Tennessee Ernest

and Patsy Cline. I hate Hank. And stupid
Incadinkadoo. I really, really, really hate
Princess. I hate. . . ."

I can never go to school again. Today Missie Fowler walked up and rubbed my back. "Just checking to see if your mom bought you a bra yet." Then she ran off giggling with her groupies. I nearly died right there in the middle of the second-floor hallway.

I couldn't even tell Sally what Missie had done because I was too embarrassed. What if Sally thinks I need a bra and just hasn't told me? Mama has always said I don't need a bra until I've got something to cover. Well, I'm not waiting any longer. Katrina's got lots of bras, so she won't miss one. There is a lot of extra space in the front though. Do you think it would be better to wear it loose or to stuff it with tube socks? I tried regular socks but they just slide right through.

Can someone grow that much overnight? Will anyone even look at me anyway? I could probably put two basketballs under my shirt and no one would notice. Why am I so plain? I want to look more like Sally, or even better, like Missie. Please don't ever let her find out I wrote this! Her head is swelled enough. Mama says pretty is as pretty does, but this saying sure doesn't work in Missie's case. She is gorgeous but as mean as a snake.

—

No one said anything today about my new and improved mature look, not even Sally. Although I think she noticed. I caught her staring at me a couple times. Do you think she could tell about the tube socks?

I tried tissues, but when I sweated they caved in and made me itch. I wonder if the kind with aloe would feel better.

I've been busted. I should have stuck the socks in at school, but instead I got careless and wore them to the breakfast table. Katrina caught me and made me take off her bra.

"You look like Dolly Parton's baby sister," she said. Then she took the pair of tube socks and put them on her feet! How embarrassing. I hope she doesn't tell Mama or even worse Bobby. He would rent space on every billboard we pass between here and school. Blabbermouth.

Was my new look that obvious? No one at school seemed to notice the difference between the new and improved me and the plain Old Venola Mae. Maybe because I sat hunched over all day with my jacket on.

I don't know what else to do. Sally and I have been doing the exercises every evening: "We MUST, we MUST, we MUST increase our BUSTS," and it is working for her. Maybe she is cheating and doing it 50 times each night instead of 25. I will try 100 tonight! Or then again maybe she is just wearing thicker tube socks.

P.S. Sally is trying out for cheerleader. Why would she want to do a stupid thing like that? We always laughed at them before.

Yikes. Grandma says I'm looking skinnier than
usual and she wants me to eat breakfast with
her in the morning. Who can eat here? I don't think
she even notices all the cat hair and the smell.

But I don't want to hurt her feelings. Maybe I
can swallow down a piece of toast. Or hide it?
Or feed it to the cats? Do cats eat toast? Can humans
get hair balls?

I'm not going to think about it. Maybe if I read
about Addie it will take my mind off E.B.T.
(Estimated Breakfast Time).

I wish I were Pippi Longstocking. She never had
a bedtime, AND if she kept a horse or a monkey
in the house, it was her choice! Even she knew
moderation, and didn't have 13 horses in the
house!

P.S. Grandma has been kind of quiet lately. I
wonder if she's feeling okay. I don't even think
she gets dressed anymore. She just leaves her
nightgown and housecoat on all day—except
Sunday when some ladies from the Women's Club
stop by to take her to church.

Oh I don't think I can bear another of Grandma's big country breakfasts. How can anyone eat with Princess clawing at your skin through the hole in the chair back or Old Blue's appearances on and across the table? He starts with one paw, then hoists himself up and saunters onto the table. By the time Granny sees him and crosses the linoleum with her fly swatter, he disappears underneath the table, waiting to perform again before his blue hair cloud settles.

If cats were sheared, they might be ugly, but they'd be a heck of a lot easier to eat breakfast with.

For Granny I've been trying to choke down toast and orange juice. I can't hurt her feelings by not eating. She's so nice to me. Yesterday she gave me money for some new school clothes even though she can't afford it, which made me feel really bad.

And today she washed and ironed the Holly Hobbie quilt for my bed. What a surprise! I walked in and there it was.

It's really pretty. You can't see the little girls' faces, but I keep imagining that one day one of them will turn around. They are probably pretty like Missy and Sally. (Sally made it for cheerleader. I wonder if she'll become like Missy. I haven't been seeing Sally as much after school, and we don't have that much to say. Do cheerleaders only talk to other cheerleaders?)

Sometimes I just don't fit in. Yesterday I told Sally that I've finally decided on "Lavender Meadow Cutright" as my new name, and she wrinkled her nose and laughed.

"Well, don't call me Nicole," she said. "It's just something immature kids do. Missy and the others have gone back to their old spellings, too." She said it's way too childish for seventh graders. (Did they grow up overnight?!?)

Almost late for school today. BOO-HOO! Gran's alarm must not have gone off. Mama had to call and wake her up.

I tried to tell Mama it was too late to catch the bus, but she helped me slap on some clothes and then drove me to school. Gee thanks.

Sometimes I can see why Grandma talks to the cats. When they rub up against her, they mean it. Even if they are after food or something, you know exactly what they want. They aren't tricky like certain people I know. Missy Fowler was nice to me in English class today, and I let her borrow some of my new lilac paper to write her homework on, and instead she used it all passing notes to Sally. With my paper! She didn't even let me know what they were giggling about. She had the nerve to ask me for another sheet for the homework, and then seemed all hurt when I gave her a plain old white sheet.

Tomorrow if she asks I might not even give her that! Or even better I could give her a sheet with a big old cat paw track on it. I've got all the ingredients.

1. Extra lilac paper
2. Cat (Baby wouldn't bite me if I picked her up. Sometimes I let her come in and curl up on my feet if they are cold.)
3. Grandma's potted peace lily (with plenty of damp dirt)

I wasted three sheets of paper with muddy prints. Missy never even asked for any today. It's like the cats tipped her off or something. But I can't be too mad because Grandma did something really special for me this morning.

She found out my weakness for hot chocolate pudding and made it . . . for BREAKFAST?!? It was kind of a nice surprise, especially since I didn't have to share it with the others.

I wonder if she might do that again sometime?

P.S. I wonder if Grandma is okay. She doesn't worry about dusting and stuff as much. I think the cats are wearing her out. I would help if she wanted me to—even though cleaning isn't my most favorite thing in the world to do.

Yes, she did it again! I woke up to the sweet smell of chocolate and dragged myself out of bed and to the table, where I sat downright mesmerized by the sway of Granny's almost KNEE-length white hair while she stirred my bubbling pudding. How can hair grow that long? Has she ever cut it in her whole lifetime? In science class we talked about whether hair and fingernails keep growing for a while once you die. Maybe mine will grow to my knees like Gran's once I'm dead.

Old Blue is getting used to me, and he seems happy under my chair, warming my toes with his in-and-out breathing and soft fur.

While I ate this morning, Granny swirled her Rapunzel-like hair into its bun for the world's inspection. I wonder if anyone but Granddad ever saw it loose and shimmering on her shoulders. I bet none of her other grandkids have.

Who would have thought that a couple of bowls of chocolate pudding could make me want to climb the hill again tonight?

Grandma and I overslept again. If I could just get Mama to do the same, I would be able to skip school for a day. Then I could watch game shows and reruns on Nickelodeon.

P.S. No time for chocolate pudding this morning. I hope Grandma wakes up on time on Monday. Maybe I should bring my own clock.

Breakfasts are going downhill!!!!!

This morning I was eating my chocolate pudding and chomped down on a rubbery hunk. Grandma forgot that my bowl had yesterday's diced onion she'd had for lunch. I didn't have the heart to tell her because she is real nice to even make it for me.

"Are you sick this morning?" she asked when she saw I had stopped eating. "If you don't want pudding, how about a piece of toast? Can't let my girl leave the house with an empty stomach."

So I did it!!! I swallowed the chocolate-covered onion bite I had in my mouth. I wouldn't do that for very many people.

All I said was, "Naw, Gran, I'm okay. Just ain't hungry."

I wasn't so sweet about the whole thing once I got home. I cried. Okay you could call it a fit. "Mama, make one of the others take a turn. Let someone else sleep with those stinkin' cats and eat a few mystery hunks."

But Mama and Daddy just said it would hurt Gran's feelings if I said I didn't want to stay, and that she wouldn't be as comfortable with my brothers around (WHO COULD BLAME HER?!?), and that Katrina couldn't possibly stay because she got home too late from her job at Pizza Hut, and about a bazillion other reasons why I was the only one qualified for the job of taking care of Granny.

Deep down, I know Mama and Daddy are torn between helping her and subjecting me to her trailer, but that doesn't help much when you're the one going to bed with the cats.

I think Katrina ratted on me for wearing her bra.
Mama asked me why I didn't talk to her about wanting
a bra. She said that maybe it was time and that
this week she was taking me to buy one that
actually fits. Wait until Missy checks the next time.
Ha!

Granny's wind-up alarm clock, or her knowing how to use it, has finally given out. She woke me up and sent me home today at 5 a.m. instead of 6:30!

I didn't mind. I'd rather sleep in my own stink-free bed anyway. I just ran down the hill and knocked real loud until Bobby opened our door. It was kind of fun to wake everybody up. (They should go to bed earlier like me, and then they wouldn't be so tired in the morning. Ha. Ha.)

Things are getting even worse at Gran's. I don't think she can smell the cats because she is with them all the time. But P-U. You can smell cat pee as soon as you get near her porch.

Mama and some people from Gran's church have been offering to help her clean, but Gran turns everybody down, takes it as an insult. She likes doing things for herself. Ugh. I'd let them clean my room in a heartbeat, as long as they didn't READ anything while they were cleaning. My journal is off limits. If you are reading this, you are in big trouble, Bobby Cutright!

I am going to start taking my baths in the morning instead of at night. Because tonight Mr. Sims, my best customer, sent an <u>Enquirer</u> home with me for Mama, and all the way home I kept smelling his cigarettes.

What if after staying at Grandma's, I'm like that newspaper and carry that cat pee smell to school with me? Maybe I smell like cat pee and no one is telling me. Surely Sally would, wouldn't she????

After all, we made the pact if there's ever any food in our teeth, or anything up our noses, or toilet paper stuck to the bottom of our shoes, we'll ALWAYS tell each other.

She would tell me about the cat pee, I think!?!

My birthday!

Mama took me to Wal-Mart and bought me my
first "training" bra. I didn't know they had to
be trained. I didn't know Mama could be so cool.
She started talking in the car about how awkward
she felt when she was my age because she was
always the tallest girl in her class, and super
skinny, too.

We really talked! And it wasn't about whether I
had done all my homework, brushed my teeth,
or hit my brother either. I didn't realize she would
understand looks and boys and stuff. It's hard
to think of your mama as being 12 once.

I told her that sometimes I feel like the geekiest,
plainest 12-year-old on the face of this earth.
You know what she did???? We were walking past
the jewelry store, and she said, "Let's just stop
in for a minute."

And when the woman said, "May I help you with
something?"

She said, "Yes, ma'am, my daughter would like
to have her ears pierced."

I have only been bugging her since I was six!!!!
I have gold studs now, but next month I can

spend my paper route money on any earrings I want. Well, not diamonds because I don't have that much money, but I'm going to buy my birthstone, which is pink, but that is okay—even though green is my favorite color.

Mama said that sometimes everyone needs help, but people won't know if we don't tell them. She says we can't be afraid to ask.

"You can ask me about ANYTHING," she said. "Maybe I can help." (I wonder if she knows about my arm shaving and the peroxide?!?)

"With six kids I can't always keep up on every little detail," she said, "but I want to help you if I can. Always." It was kind of cool, like a Brady Bunch moment.

Then when I got here tonight, Grandma gave me two pillow shams she'd quilted especially for MY birthday. Each has three Holly Hobbie girls on the front and three on the back. Twelve Holly Hobbies because I am 12! I wonder if she thought about that. She used lilac, baby blue, candy apple green, pink, and yellow material—just like her quilt. They are the most beautiful things I've owned in my whole life. Should I keep them on my bed at home or here where they match the quilt??? Or maybe one at each place?

P.S. Sally brought over a present for me today. She said even though she's a cheerleader, she is still my best friend. (That was present enough, but the makeup kit she gave me is cool, too.) We talked Mama into letting me keep it. "As long as you don't go to school looking like a clown," she said. YAHOO!

It happened again!! Gran's still having problems with her alarm clock. But this time she woke me up and fed me breakfast in the middle of the night. Then she put me out the door for school. It was still dark out and I knew it was kind of early. "Did I even go to sleep at all?" I wondered as I walked down the hill through the cold, wet grass.

EVEN WORSE no amount of pounding on the door woke my family, so I figured I'd just sit down on the porch until Daddy got up to go to work. Granny's lights were out and she was back in bed, probably with angelic Princess curled up on her feet. (Maybe Princess is messing with the clock to get even with me for throwing that glass of cold water on her the other night in the bathroom. She definitely has it in for me. Why can't she be more like Baby or Old Blue?)

So I sat down in the porch swing and waited. I kept waiting and waiting and it didn't get daylight. And Daddy didn't get up to go to work. That's when I started to catch on that it WAS still night. So I spent last night in the porch swing, hating the world and everyone who was sleeping in it, and wishing an escaped convict would stop by and murder me just to make everybody feel bad. Poor Old Blue, who must have escaped from Granny's when I left, got the worst of my anger. Sidling up next to me just wasn't a smart thing to try right then.

When Daddy opened the door and found me asleep in the porch swing, I could tell he didn't know whether to laugh or yell. But then Mama and Daddy started arguing about Gran, so I went to my room and back to sleep until it was time to get up for school.

Mama and Daddy are still arguing about what to do about Gran. Mama pretty much says, "She's your mother," and Daddy said, "How would you feel if she was your mama."

I don't like to see them upset.

When I left, Mama kissed me on the cheek and said, "You're being a really great kid about this. Just hang in there a little longer until we can come up with a better plan." Her eyes looked like she had been crying. I hope not.

"I'm doing okay," I said. But I didn't want her to quit hugging me.

Things are definitely getting worse. The furry little felines are winning the war. Fleas are no longer just something I worry about. I've been seeing things hop around on the bed. I saw one just now! I felt something crawling on me, and when I went to swipe it off, it jumped and disappeared.

I caught it and squished it with my fingernails. (My nails are finally long enough to squeeze a flea now because I am trying to let them grow. Sally says it is unsanitary and "neurotic" to bite them. My nails, not the fleas. But I wouldn't bite a flea either because the one I squished had blood in it. My blood!)

I itch all over.

My ankle stings.

Something is biting me.

I just saw another FLEA.

I don't want to stay.

I'm calling Mama.

I'll tell Grandma my stomach hurts. She won't mind spending just the rest of tonight alone, will she?

I hope the fleas don't eat HER alive.

I just want to go HOME.

Mama took Grandma to the doctor for her checkup today, and I was right, she is not okay. The doctor says her sugar is EXTREMELY high, and so he admitted her to the hospital until they can get it under control.

P.S. I don't know why <u>her</u> sugar is high. I am the one who eats all the chocolate pudding. She just eats toast. (Last Saturday I ate a whole can of Betty Crocker's frosting.) I always crave chocolate. Maybe I should get my sugar checked, too.

Went to see Grandma in the hospital.

She said, "Venola Mae, just the person I wanted
to see. Will you feed my cats until I can get out
of this place?"

"Sure, Gran," I said. I couldn't believe she trusted
me more than anyone else with her babies.

"Princess, too?" she asked. "I know you two
aren't on the best of terms."

"Yeah, Gran. Even Princess."

That's when Gran started talking out of her head.
"Maybe Princess would like to sleep with you at
your house until I get home. She would probably
enjoy a little vacation."

My eyes almost bugged out of their sockets
before I realized she was teasing. Even though
she looks really weak, she still has a pretty good
sense of humor.

P.S. I love Grandma, but I hope she never ever
thinks I'm sleeping with Princess!

Grandma is diabetic, and once she comes home, she has to get her sugar checked and take shots before every meal.

What if they ask me to give her shots? I turn green at the sight of needles even if they are on TV programs. Ahhhhh.

Mama and Daddy were arguing about Grandma again. Daddy thinks she should move in with us.

Mama said, "Fine, I love your mother. But not the cats. One maybe, but 13? Forget it!"

I wish things could go back to the way they were before Grandma got sick. I thought I would be really happy not to have to stay with the cats anymore, but now I feel rotten instead.

Mama and Daddy invited Grandma to move in with them today.

I think Gran knew that even though she was invited, all 13 cats wouldn't be welcome, so she told Mama and Daddy she really preferred having her own place.

"I think I can manage by myself. Maybe not as well as before, but the doctor says there's a home health program and nurses will stop in and give me my shots until I catch on. And if I want someone to stay nights, they have volunteers for that, too."

I can't believe it. Doesn't Grandma want ME anymore?!?

We went to visit Grandma again tonight. I told
her the cats are fine, and she told me where the
money is to buy more cat food. Maybe I'll get them
some treats with my own money. They are
probably pretty sad.

"Will you do me one more favor?" she asked.

"Sure, what Gran?" I asked, hoping she wasn't
going to bring up the whole "Princess-needs-a-
vacation thing" again.

"How about taking that Holly Hobbie quilt down
to your house for me? I think it would like to be
with your pillow shams."

I couldn't believe it. She <u>was</u> getting rid of me.

"Are you kicking me out for good, Grandma?"

Grandma laughed. "Of course not. You'll always
be welcome to visit any time you want, but I
think you should stay at home evenings and
concentrate on doing your math homework and
cleaning your room, and things."

Did Mama and Daddy show her the C– I got on
my report card??? Or did they tell her you have
to crawl over stuff to find my bed?!? I hope not. I
don't want her to think I am a total slob.

Katrina is jealous because Grandma didn't give her a quilt OR even a pillow sham. Tee hee.

I'm not sure the quilt will be the same though. I'll miss Baby on my feet. He is really, really warm, and lately he has been curling up on my stomach sometimes.

School is same. Paper route is same. But I miss Baby. And Grandma. Not Princess.

Reverend Lawson mentioned Grandma at the beginning of his service today.

"Brothers and Sisters," he said, "Lily Cutright is temporarily in the hospital battling to get her diabetes under control. Please remember her in your prayers today. Illness not only affects the individual but the entire family. So say a prayer of comfort for Lily's children and grandchildren, too, who are showering her with love and devotion during this trying time."

I wonder if Reverend Lawson meant for everyone to pray for Gran's cats, too? Maybe I should teach him their names so he can make sure the congregation doesn't miss one in their prayers.

P.S. A prayer or two sure couldn't hurt nasty old Princess.

P.P.S. I wonder if Reverend Lawson does exorcisms. Tee hee.

Missy came up to me to do her regular bra check, and boy was she surprised. Ha. Ha. It snapped really loud, and she got sent to the principal by Mrs. Stemple for being "unruly." Ha. Ha. Ha.

Sally told Missy she needed to grow up. She wrote me a note that said Missy is immature, and that she wouldn't even speak to her if she wasn't a "fellow" cheerleader.

P.S. Grandma might get to come home tomorrow if she keeps improving.

Instead of just following me and calling me goofy names, Sammy helped me with my route today. We found a gangly gray teenage kitten behind the Hi/Lo Dumpster. Its ribs show, and Sammy said it reminds him of me.

It was definitely starving, so we stuck it in my newspaper bag, and took it to my house and fed it some milk. I also gave it some treats that I had saved back for the next time I see Baby. I think I might let it stay. I asked Mama and she said it was okay, as long as I didn't get all silly and bring home 13 of them. If Grandma taught me anything, it is MODERATION!

I am going to name her Tiger Lily.

P.S. They are keeping Grandma one more night, but she gets to come home for sure tomorrow and I can introduce her to Tiger then.

P.P.S. Gran has finally decided to take Mama up on our offer to help her clean her trailer. Well, for me, Mama, and Katrina to help. She doesn't believe in boys or men doing housework. So the three of us are going to help her on Saturdays and Wednesday evenings. But while we clean HER house, Daddy and my brothers have to clean our house because Mama is a modern-day woman who DOES believe in boys and men doing housework. Double tee hee!

Grandma's home! She says Tiger Lily is a fine cat name and has invited both of us to a pajama party this coming weekend.

Princess better not be snobby to MY CAT, or we might just not take her any treats the next time.

P.S. Now that Grandma's all right and I'm back home, things are pretty much back to normal around here. Dad's snoring rattles the windows. My brothers hog the TV and burp all the time. And today, Katrina got all mad because I was sneaking out the back door in her new silk blouse. (I was just going to borrow it for an hour to wear on the paper route and then put it back.) Ahh, home sweet home.